Your Family Tree

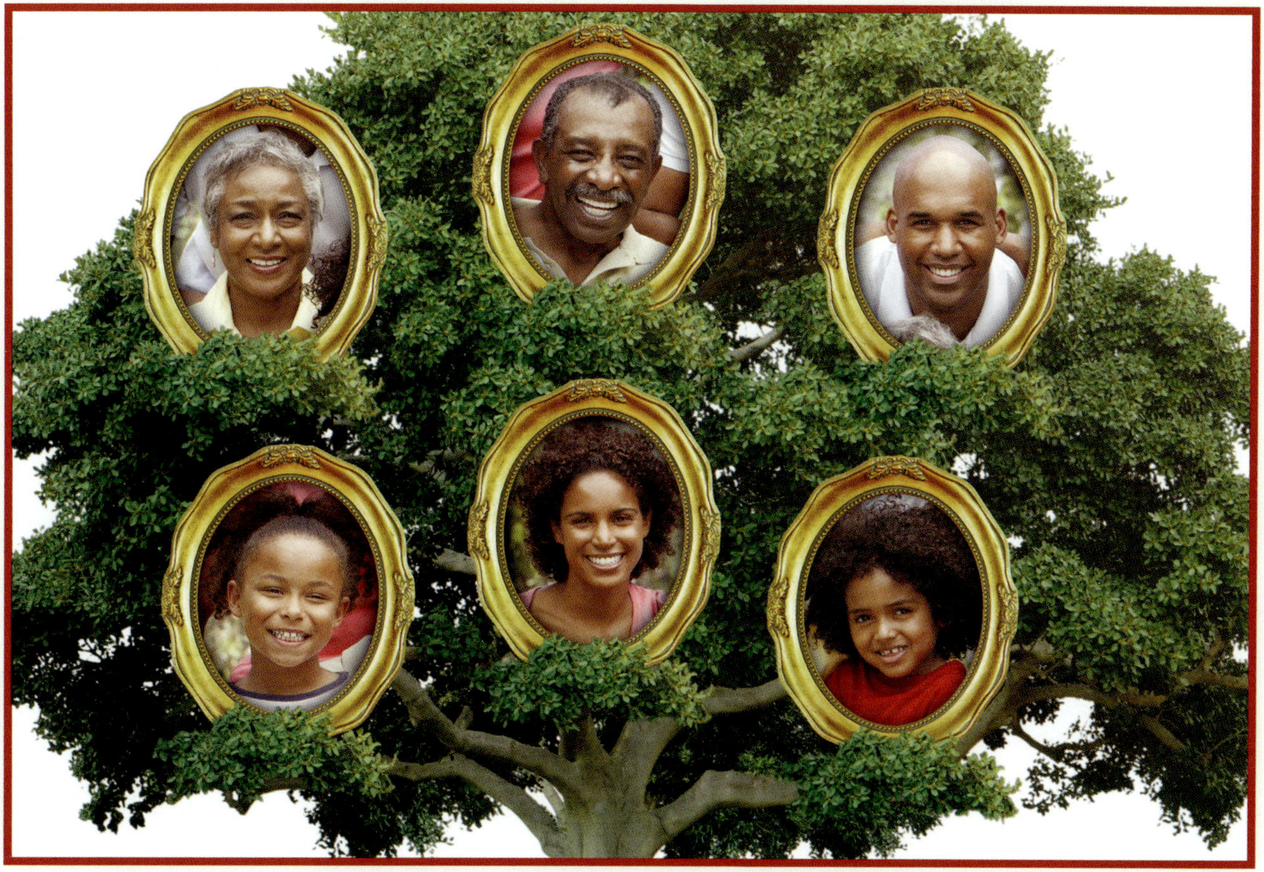

Written by Robin Koontz

rourkeeducationalmedia.com

Scan for Related Titles and Teacher Resources

© 2014 Rourke Educational Media

All rights reserved. No part of this book may be reproduced or utilized in any form or by any means, electronic or mechanical including photocopying, recording, or by any information storage and retrieval system without permission in writing from the publisher.

www.rourkeeducationalmedia.com

PHOTO CREDITS: Cover & title page: © Monkey Business Images, @ DNY59: © OCAL; page 3: © Juri Samsonov; page 4: © Monkey Business Images; page 5: © Ajay Bhaskar, © Rohit Seth; page 7: © manley099; page 9: © Andriy Popov, © YinYang; page 11: © Patrick Poendl; page 12: © Ron Chapple; page 13: © Jani Bryson; page 15: © szefei; page 16: Blend Images; page 17: © Anna Lurye; page 19

Edited by: Jill Sherman

Cover by: Tara Raymo

Interior design by: Pam McCollum

Library of Congress PCN Data

Your Family Tree / Robin Koontz
(Little World Social Studies)
ISBN 978-1-62169-917-0 (hard cover)(alk. paper)
ISBN 978-1-62169-812-8 (soft cover)
ISBN 978-1-62717-022-2 (e-Book)
Library of Congress Control Number: 2013937311

Also Available as:

Rourke Educational Media
Printed in the United States of America,
North Mankato, Minnesota

Rourke Educational Media

rourkeeducationalmedia.com
customerservice@rourkeeducationalmedia.com • PO Box 643328 Vero Beach, Florida 32964

Table of Contents

A Family Tree 4

Tracing History 8

Passing it Down 14

A Family Forest 18

Glossary 22

Index 24

Websites 24

About the Author 24

A Family Tree

A **family** is a lot like a tree. A seed sprouts and a tree begins to grow. Soon, the tree grows branches. The branches grow leaves. As time passes, the tree sprouts more branches and leaves.

On a family tree, the leaves are family members. The branches show how the family members are related. A new leaf sprouts when a new person joins the family.

This family tree shows one kind of family.

Tracing History

A family tree traces family history. As family members are added, a family tree grows.

Your family tree will grow when babies are born into the family. It will grow when children are adopted. It will grow even more when people get married.

A family tree can trace hundreds of years of family history. It is a written record of who your parents, grandparents, and great grandparents were.

Some families stay in the same place for a long time. Other families have members all over the world. No matter where people live, they are connected by a family tree.

Family members who were born before your grandparents are your **ancestors**. They may have **immigrated** to the place your family lives today.

Millions of people have immigrated to the United States. They wanted to start a new life in a new place.

Passing it Down

People **inherit** lots of things from their ancestors. It could be land or family treasures. It could also be the color of their hair or skin, the size of their nose, or even the way they behave!

We inherit how we look from our parents and their ancestors.

People also get family **traditions** from their ancestors. Families pass special traditions down to their children.

Traditions, land, treasured objects, and ways of living are all parts of a family's **heritage**.

A family tradition can be a cookie recipe, a song, or even a game. Ask your family and friends about their traditions. Add those traditions to your family tree.

A Family Forest

There are lots of ways to trace family history. It's not always easy. A lot of family history is hard to find. A good way to learn about your family history is by asking questions.

When you have gathered information, you can build your own family tree.

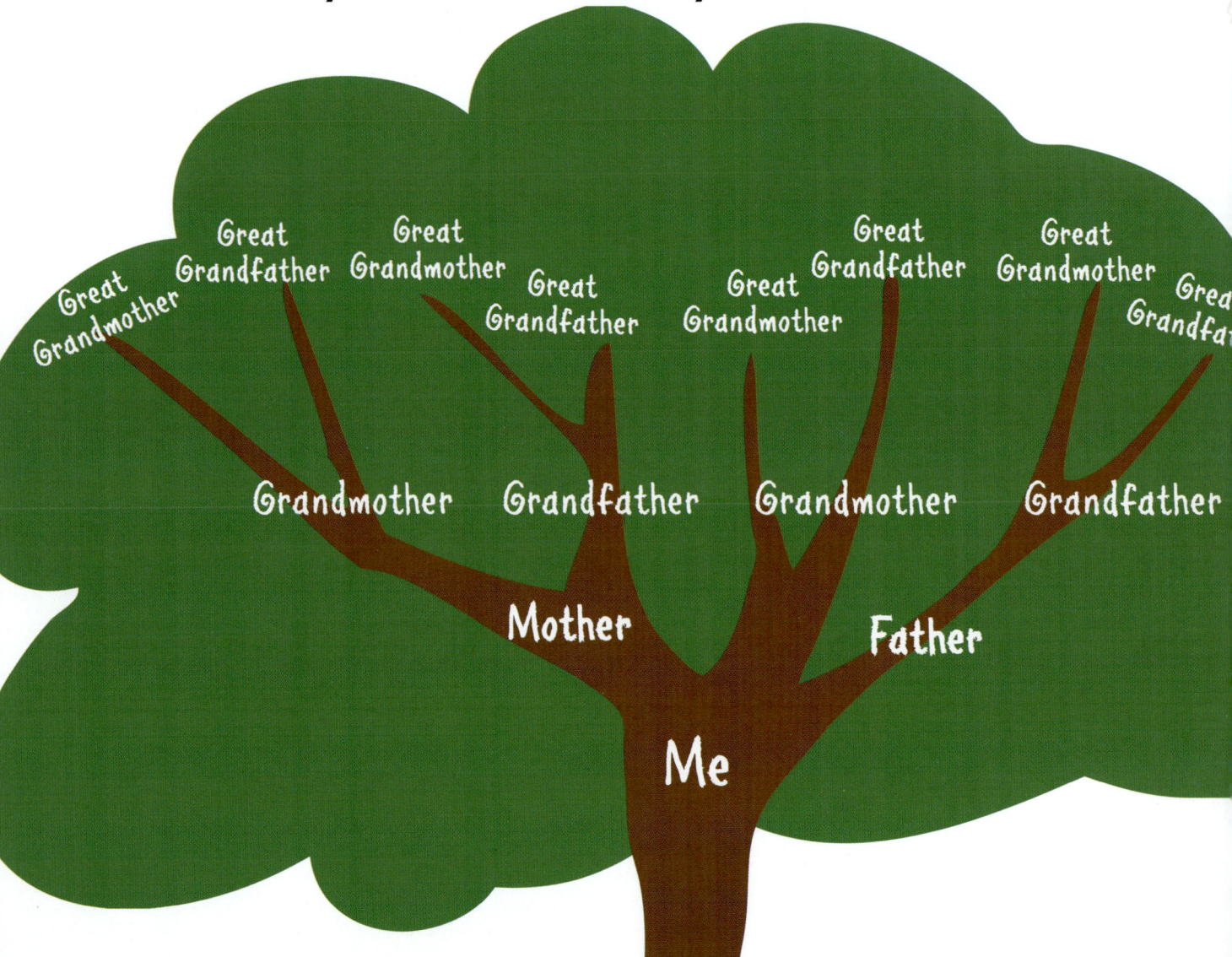

The world is a forest of family trees that links all people together. We can learn about family histories by sharing our family trees with each other.

Picture Glossary

 **ancestors** (an-CESS-tuhrz): Ancestors are the people we come from. They are the parents and grandparents of our grandparents.

 **family** (FAM-ih-lee): A family is a group of related people. It can include parents, sisters, and brothers.

 **heritage** (HARE-ih-tij): Heritage is what comes from someone's background.

 **immigrated** (im-uh-GRAYTD): To immigrate is to come to live in a new country.

 **inherit** (in-HARE-it): Someone inherits when they receive something from their parents or ancestors.

 **traditions** (trah-DISH-uhnz): A tradition is a belief or custom that is passed from parents to children.

Index

ancestors 12, 14, 15
family 4, 6, 8, 10, 12, 14, 16, 18, 20, 21
heritage 16
history 8, 10, 18
immigrated 12, 13
inherit 14, 15
tradition(s) 16, 17

Websites

kids.familytreemagazine.com/kids/default.asp

www.familytreetemplates.net/category/kids

www.genwriters.com/children.html

About the Author

Robin Koontz is an author and illustrator of a wide variety of books and articles for children and young adults. She lives with her husband in the Coast Range of western Oregon.

Meet The Author!
www.meetREMauthors.com